Larceny & Love

Ima Ghoul

The Written Word Publishing

Contents

Author Note

This story is written using Australian English and grammar. There will be several differences compared to US English but these differences are correct under Australian English standards.

Content Warning

This story is purely fictional and contains fantasy violence. While the story includes mild nudity there is nothing graphic as it is a closed-door romance. Any prejudice towards the main characters exists to portray the types of bullying Ima Ghoul is against. In no way does this story glorify harassment of any kind but encourages people to recognise how it impacts others and stand against such occurrences.

Chapter One

It wasn't pleasant weather for anyone to be working in; thunder rumbled amongst the grey storm clouds spontaneously interrupted by streaks of lightning, rudely disrupting the shadows that conceal me. I brush my wet hair out of my eyes; my stomach grumbles, reminding me of the hunger I have been trying to ignore. The deluge of icy rain continues to try its best to drown me, as if the rain gods have made me their sworn enemy. The lengths a girl has to go to in order to eat these days is shocking. As the last flash of lightning passes, I make a run towards my mark, withdrawing my dagger from my belt, my heart thuds dully in my chest, my breath quickening.

My mark stumbles blindly into the alleyway from the tavern I had just exited moments ago. His companions laugh and wave him off as they gambol in opposing directions, surely homeward bound. I lick my lips; soon I will be able to eat. That purse must have been full, the treasures within so easily spent on beer and bread. Surely he can spare a little for a hungry stranger?

The nobleman tips his hat to some people passing by and begins to whistle; occasionally launching into raucous singing. 'I got paid, pennies in my pocket. Time to get me a bottle of ale, the finest in town and share in song and bread with me mates. Oh Shaol, a home so fine, I'm glad you are mine.'

The noble belches and I role my eyes at the poorly written sea shanty, an ode to our fishing village of Shaol, a veritable cesspool of ne'er-do-wells, unemployed former fishermen, veterans and thriving nobles.

When the wars between the human Kingdom of Rersherdia and the fae kingdom of Valdarn took place thirty years ago, many resources were depleted. Both sides used experimental magic and poisoned our world's natural resources. Food is scarce and larceny is almost, but not quite a mainstream career. Still, it's not something you would brag about at family dinners, but less alarming and taboo than being one of the Velshere.

The mark stumbles and retches; the smell of vomit makes me cover my nose as I creep closer. My eyes narrow on the purse. Lifting my dagger, I slice through the threads holding it on the belt, freezing as it plops into my palm and emits an unexpected, ear-piercing shriek. I turn on my heel and bolt, my worn boots sliding in the wet, and I drop my dagger.

'Wait.'

As if I would. I grin and put distance between myself and my victim. Scampering around a corner, I lean against a wall. Patrons at a nearby eatery huddle together under the lean-to scattered with small stools. A woman ladles stew into wooden bowls from a cauldron balanced over a tripod on a banked coal fire. The pale lamplight from the lanterns attached to the overhang of the little stall is a welcome reprieve from the darkness in my life.

The smell of Furrcon, a local delicacy, makes my mouth water and my breath steams in the air. I dip my hand into the pouch and yelp as something sharp latches onto my right wrist, wincing, the bag shrieks again as I try to wrench it from my aching appendage.

My gaze snaps up, landing on the sapphire-robed noble as he hurries into the alleyway. He gives me a wicked grin. Anger boils up within and I clench my left hand ready to punch that smug expression off his handsome face.

'The guards will come soon. Best let me remove that for you.' His green eyes lock on my carnelian-coloured ones. 'He mentioned you were Velshere.'

A woman screams and points to me. 'Look, a monster.'

I grit my teeth and rush my former mark, shouldering him to the left. I almost make it past when his hand moves too fast for comfort, grips the collar of my grey blouse and flings me into a nearby brick wall. The air is knocked from my lungs, and as I draw in a heaving breath, he runs his hand over my left wrist. 'Do you have a name?'

My mind is distracted from someone willing to touch me and my thoughts race haphazardly around my mind. It has been nigh on a year since that willingly occurred. 'Rue,' I mumble a hasty pseudonym.

'*Falgor remarda.*' The man strokes my contained wrist, his hands are strong and warm, lingering just a little too long.

His gaze focuses on my mouth and, when I bite my lips, his jaw clenches. I feel my cheeks heat and I glance away. The bag chitters in reply to the noble's unfamiliar words.

'What language was that?'

'Valdarnish.' He grins. 'Now, Rue, why did you steal from me?'

'I was hungry.' I try to pull my hand away. 'Not that it matters, you were an easy target, and I am hardly the worst you will meet in a dark alley.'

Seemingly unaffected from our encounter he drops his hand. The purse chitters again before slipping off my wrist. My brows arch in surprise as tiny blinking red eyes appear and the former bag lands on the ground and sprouts diminutive orange legs. The strange thing hisses at me before lunging. I stumble back.

'What did I do to you?'

The robed man frowns at his pet. '*Falgor remarda!*'

The creature whimpers and quietens as he leans down and scoops it up. It is covered in coarse, frizzy hair; the same, I assume, makes up the pouch to hold items. Fuzzy strands begin to weave themselves around its owner's belt, attaching itself securely to the noble.

My heart skips a beat as the sound of booted feet near the alleyway makes me turn my head in that direction. 'They went down here.'

'Please,' I whisper and bite my lip. 'They can't capture me.'

My captor nods. His eyes are bleary and he turns to block my escape. Two guards, dressed in Shaol guard uniforms consisting of hide caps and grey leather breastplates decorated with golden flying fish, enter the alleyway.

One stomps towards us. 'What happened here?'

The robed man spreads his arms wide. 'Whatever do you mean, officer?'

The guard's eyes widen and lock on the nobleman's before he bows in the middle. 'Lord Asherton. Forgive the intrusion.'

They turn to leave and that annoying woman from before screams again. 'Velshere behind him.'

The guard turns back towards us and his gaze flitters from the screaming woman's to Asherton's. 'Best we look. We don't won't any of the nefarious Velshere at large in Shaol.'

My hands shake and I back away. 'No, they will imprison me or experiment on me.'

A few customers toss their bowls at me and my lip quivers as I squash down the urge to cry as scalding liquid burns my right hand. I slap the bowls away and they clatter to the ground.

'Why are the Velshere so feared in human cities?' Asherton steps towards the guards. 'Because of insidious gossip? Why hate the offspring of a human and fae?'

'We no naught of their capabilities,' a patron mutters.

'Fae come in so many forms including dangerous ones. How can we know what we are getting?' someone else shouts.

'That sounds like ignorance and an excuse to bully. Look how malnourished she looks. Can no one spare some empathy?' Asherton turns towards me and holds out his hand and his eyes soften. 'Come.'

I hesitate, backing further away and stumble over a crack in the pavement.

'*Remarda cevere.*' When Asherton says those words, an innate thrill goes through me, and some ancient memory buried deep below the surface flashes across my mind for a fraction of a second, I reach out and clasp his hand.

A guard pushes past my protector with his club raised to strike.

'No!' Asherton steps forward and punches the guard in the nose. Blood spurts from the injured man's face as the other guard surges up behind my would-be hero.

I scream as the guard raises her weapon and toss a stool towards my assailant, distracting her long enough so I can slip past. As I try to flee, a patron puts out their foot and

I flounder, hissing through my teeth at the villager. With a dull thud the guard's weapon glances off my skull, pain spreads throughout my left temple as my sight becomes hazy at best.

As I flounder about I throw out my arms. 'Help me please.' Laughter from people in the crowd presses in on me. Warm blood trickles down my cheek. Soon, darkness and its familiar loneliness greets me and takes away my pain.

Chapter Two

I snuggle down under the covers, savouring the warmth that I last felt what seems a lifetime ago. This is a prison? The room is sparse but clean, lit with two candles fitted in brackets either side of the wooden door. The undecorated walls appear to be made of limestone; a deep contrast to the slate floor. But this bed is something else, made of rich mahogany and could easily accommodate three people.

The stuffed mattress smells of hay and sweet-smelling dried herbs and flowers. It is bedecked with soft pillows and thick blankets. I stretch and throw back the covers, sliding the floor. My bare feet connect with the cold surface and I wriggle my toes to keep them warm before padding over to a solitary dresser adorned with a dusty mirror.

Wincing, I turn my head; my fair skin near my left ear is festooned with a large dark bruise. I stare down at my new clothes; my threadbare blouse, boots and breeches have been replaced with a simple long-sleeved shift. At least

I have retained my under things. My cheeks burn with indignity; somebody has removed my clothes.

I clench my jaw. How could someone do that? A feeling of unease washes over me and I shudder. I take a deep breath, trying to calm myself and remember the state they had been in and how cold and wet I had felt. They had probably saved me from sickness or even death from the cold, but it is still unnerving.

I pull open the drawers and start rummaging around, searching for anything that could aid my escape. I sneeze as a cloud of dust drifts towards me from the excessive motion. I am rewarded with very little: a hair pin, some crumpled paper, a sole earring. Heck, I probably can't even pick the lock on the door with any of these, the pin is too brittle. Why are these things in a prison of all places? My mind drifts to the fanciful; perhaps some lone princess was locked away here awaiting marriage to a cruel prince. He never came and she succumbed to her fate. My stomach upsets my deluded daydream by grumbling loudly.

The door handle turns and I snatch up the pin, sliding it up my sleeve as the door swings open. A guard rushes in.

'Step away from the dresser, your back to the wall.'

I hurry to comply, and she slaps a copper tray on to the dresser; the contents of the bowl sloshing about. As the guard hurries out of the room, the sound of the key turning in the lock makes me glance towards the door. I meander over to the tray; on it a wooden bowl, a wooden cup with water and hunk of bread. I dip the bread into the green stew and cram it in my mouth; the salty, fishy broth does wonders for a woman's spirit.

Furrcon is the common fare served often in Shaol; comforting and nutritious, made from seaweed, fish stock and salt. The stew is sometimes served with hunks of fish and is our national dish. No dessert? Very unusual, as it is usually served with every meal and to not do so is against our traditions. So much so that our country holds an annual sweet competition; the victor is rewarded greatly and they are seen as a national treasure, the title handed down to their offspring. Our sugar cane farmers take great pride, and sugar cane grows quite well in our sandy soil. Our biggest trade is seaweed, shellfish, copper products, sweets and rum.

Surrounded by a silver ocean, our land is covered in craggy caves, home to dangerous monsters who hassle bornite miners, and is the number one cause of death for humankind. I gulp. Will I end up working in one of the mines to pay my dues? Large parties of prison miners often attract the most beastly of creatures.

Those tunnels also hold vast fortunes from smugglers who trade in secret with the fae lands. One of these days I will explore some of those caverns on my own, keeping far away from beastly things. I will take what I need to set myself up so I will never be hungry again.

I finish my meal and hurry over to the door. This is less of a prison and more like a bedroom in an inn or house and should be easy enough to escape from if I can get the door unlocked. I grip the handle and turn; the door refuses to open. I shrug and slip the pin inside the lock, applying a bit of force which causes my tool to snap.

The handle jiggles in my hands as pressure is exerted from the other side, I stub my toe. 'Ouch!'

I take a step back as the guard from before glares at me and enters to retrieve my tray. Standing just outside the doorway is the nobleman and a plain-clothed woman.

The woman steps into the room and Asherton follows as the guard with the tray steps past me and into the hall-way.

'Are you sure?' The plain-clothed woman's brow furrows.

Asherton reaches out, and I flinch, before he pats me on the shoulder. 'See, she knows me.'

I am tempted to bite his hand and his companion turns towards me. 'I am investigator Dawson. When you arrived I processed you and have washed your belongings. I and a female officer changed you and brought you to this room.'

Asherton pipes up. 'At my expense. I use this room when I am in Shaol. We are in the Fishslop Inn.'

I shift my feet. 'Where are the terrible dungeons and torture apparatus? I am one of the Velshere after all.'

Dawson blinks in surprise. 'All interred persons are treated as innocent until their case is investigated. Hard labour is the preferred punishment in the most severe cases and we are opposed to extreme force. I assume you are not from the isles and maybe from the mainland of the fae?'

I shake my head. 'I was born just outside of Shaol. My mother is alive.

'Then why are you stealing from citizens?' The investigator frowns.

I shrug. 'I never said she was well. My mother is sick and food is scarce.'

The guard glares at me from outside the doorway. 'Food is scarce for most since the war and our lack of trade and banishment from Valdarn is affecting everyone. You should see what it's like in the capital for the majority. Very little variety. Scarcity does not give you an excuse to steal.'

I sigh. I have always wanted to visit the glittering city of Silver Waters, but I have never had enough coin to outfit myself for the journey. I frown. If they are opposed to violence how can they explain my treatment? I point to my injury. 'I was treated violently.'

Dawson nods. 'I am aware. The guard has been reprimanded and fined.' She holds out a small purse. I open the brown drawstring bag and count out sixteen copper square-shaped chips, each piece has a fish embossed on the surface and is stamped with a large R; the coins are known as Rurrs.

'This is a generous sum.' I push them back into the bag and shove the pouch into the pocket of my shift.

'Your compensation.' Dawson gestures to Asherton. 'We have housed you in his room. You were going to be sentenced to six months of hard labour, but he insists you are his betrothed.'

My mouth drops open and I snap it shut. 'What? He's lying.'

Asherton puts his finger to his lips but I glare at him. 'I hate liars.'

His eyes widen and he smirks. 'As opposed to thieves?'

Dawson frowns. 'I will have her removed from your custody immediately and escorted to the town boundaries where she will be free to go. In the future do not lie to us.'

The guard hands Asherton the tray; her booted feet thud dully across the slate as she reaches for me and pulls my back towards her torso before my wrists are clamped in manacles.

As I am turned towards him, I hold my head up high only to meet his eyes, which dance with merriment. 'I wish to pursue charges.'

'What?' I spit out.

Dawson snatches the contents from my pocket and tosses the bag to my host. 'That is almost enough for the fine.'

Asherton counts the coins slowly in his palm, his mouth set in a wicked grin. 'Twelve short, I believe.'

The investigator frowns. 'That's at least a month of hard labour. And this is her first offence.'

'So be it.' I stare down the nobleman.

'As far as you know. She hasn't been caught yet, that makes her a professional thief.' Asherton shrugs. 'Let's see how long she can take it.' He steps forward and brushes my shoulder with his hand; I snap my teeth at him. 'She's not a very strong looking person.'

Visions of kneeing him in vulnerable areas keep me merry as I am escorted from the room.

Chapter Three

I wipe the sweat off my brow with the back of my hand, pausing as the sun beats down on me from its zenith in the sky. Leaning against the large steel hammer clasped in my right hand, I breathe deeply, taking a reprieve from breaking large rocks. Six hours in and I am exhausted; my breakfast was little more than course brown bread and warm milk.

'Get back to it,' a fellow inmate mutters.

'Yeah, they will halve our rations if they catch you being lazy. And that's the sixth break you've had this hour, Velshere.' Another scowls at me.

A gong sounds denoting the hour's passing.

'Lunch time,' shouts a female guard.

'Oh, I'm looking forward to this.' The prisoner next to me tosses down her tool and spits on her raw and calloused hands as if she is trying to cool the tender, harried flesh.

A group of prisoners hurry over to the wooden picnic tables and take their seat as others dressed in well-worn navy aprons begin to hand out mugs and tin plates. Another prisoner carries a pot and ladle and begins ladling the contents onto the plates.

I push myself into a remaining seat and reach for the teapot in front of me; the person next to me growls and slaps my hand away. 'No tea for Velshere scum.'

The woman opposite me, her eyes on her meal of boiled vegetables and meat, mutters back. 'Careful, you don't know what powers she has.'

I scowl; should I tell them I am not a threat and my gifts never manifested? No, I could use this to my advantage and begin to sing a nursery rhyme someone had once sang at my crib.

'We dwelt under a lightless sky once prey to the creatures that dwelleth there.' I stare past the woman who had slapped me and snort derisively before turning a wide-eyed gaze towards her. 'Buggity boo.'

The prisoner beside me gasps, her eyes flit to mine and the teapot. Her hand shaking, she hastily fills my mug with the sweet-smelling tea. 'Are you cursing me?'

I smirk. 'Maybe.'

She scoops up her plate and empties the contents on to mine and turns away from me. I reach for the common coarse brown bread and use it to shovel my meal into my mouth; it is unseasoned but warming and I am ravenous. I finish my meal quickly and washing it down with the sugary, hot black tea.

After the meal things are cleared away. My small prison troop of four exchanges positions with the crushers and the afternoon is filled with shoving rocks into the machine. As I turn the handle, another prisoner dumps a bucket of smaller stones into the crusher. I am met with extensive resistance, requiring all the strength I have left. The cogs screech and the the teeth crush the rocks into smaller pieces. A prisoner sounds the gong six times and I stare up at the sky; the sun has dropped below the horizon.

'Finish up, ladies.'

My shoulders droop wearily and I follow the others back to the cells. Upon entry to the building we remove our yellow jumpsuits and toss them in a basket to be washed, leaving us in our linen shifts.

Lining up in single file, my fellow inmates wash their face and hands with the soap and water bucket provided. I am last; the water is murky, grime coating the rim of the bucket. As exhaustion washes over me, I give it little thought as I scrub myself lightly with the rough carbolic soap that smells faintly of disinfectant. Afterwards I shuffle into the cell behind my cell mates. As the steel door slams shut, I flop down on the packed dirt floor and reach for the holy blanket.

'Hey, Velshere, can you get us out?'

'Yeah, use your magic.'

Fear tingles along my spine and I remain quiet, my body tense and ready to react should I need to. 'I am too tired to use it.'

'Maybe she is lying to us,' says the woman who had slapped my hand away at lunch.

I gasp as someone stands over me; the dim light from the small window shrouds my cellmate in darkness before she boots me in the stomach. I groan before shuffling back against the wall. The others rush towards me, their fists raised. They strike me repeatedly; the pain is blinding and I put my hands up to protect my face. The sound of the door screeching open causes the blows to stop.

'Enough!' The masculine voice filled with rage makes me drop my hands and my attackers pull away. Asherton stands glaring at my cell mates as a guard with a torch enters the chamber and drags me through the opening.

'Why are you here?' I rush out, forcing myself to take shallow breaths as I try not to exacerbate the ache in my ribs.

Dawson turns the corner and hurries over to us. 'What happened here?'

'I came to collect the coins the prisoner earned to pay off the fine.' Asherton gestures to me. 'Her cell mates beat her for being Velshere.'

Dawson sighs and steps past us. 'Take the Velshere and go, she is not safe here. I saw nothing, my lord.'

'Wait, I refuse to be in debt to this man.' I shrug my shoulders and the guard drops her hands.

'You will go without food tomorrow,' Dawson says to the prisoners.

Asherton leans down and pulls me up against his hard chest. I slap his elbow away; his arms dropping to his side and I take a step back and glower at him. He chuckles before his hand flashes out and grabs my chin; his firm grip forces my face towards my fellow prisoners. 'Such bravery.'

'Let me at the traitorous Velshere.' One of my cellmates reaches through the bars, her face a mask of pure hate. 'I'll kill her.'

My eyes widen and Asherton's breath is warm on my face and smells of mint and ale. 'Them or me. Choose. I, at least, won't hurt you.'

I push his hand away. 'Why are you doing this?'

He stands at his full height, a good foot taller than me, and shrugs. 'I'll explain later.'

'Arrrgh.' Another of my cellmates rushes the bars and I take a deep breath. 'Sure, let's go.'

Asherton nods and releases my chin before snatching up my arm. I lean into him as he meanders down the passageway towards the stairwell that will take me away from this prison.

As I climb the stairs with his assistance, I take in a deep breath as moonlight washes over me. Never have I known such pain, both emotionally and physically. My lip quivers as I try to hold back unshed tears. As my bare feet touch the sand outside the prison, a burning sensation begins in my toes and rushes through my veins; my blood is on fire, yet my breath is like ice in my lungs. My eyes lock on to Asherton's, his are wide with awe.

'Beautiful.' He steps towards me.

The moon seems to swell. There is a flash of light before I am bathed in moonlight. The light is extinguished as dark, ominous clouds drift across the moon's face. I am tempted to weep; the moon's presence was often my only consolation during my lonely childhood. Exhaustion overtakes me and I falter.

Asherton rushes towards me, and he scoops me up into his broad, strong arms. 'I've got you, *Cevere.*'

Those words comfort me as he hurries out of the prison gates. A horse drawn carriage clatters by and he avoids a clump of manure on the road. He whistles loudly and the driver pulls up nearby, leaps down from the carriage and pulls open the door. One of the two chestnut horses stamps its feet and nickers.

'Twenty-three Fishluck Lane.' Asherton shoves me into the carriage and hops in behind me. As the door clicks shut, I lean back against the leather seat as the vehicle sways and gathers speed.

'So, what now?'

Asherton smiles. 'Is this the first time you've been caught?'

I nod.

'Well, I am in need of a professional thief. Are you opposed to revenge in the name of love?'

I lean forward. 'Intriguing.'

Chapter Four

The carriage pulls up outside a manor house in various states of disrepair. As we alight from the vehicle, Asherton hands over my former compensation purse to the driver. I scowl as the carriage pulls away; a flurry of dust swirls around our feet.

My companion shrugs. 'I had to pay the man.'

'With my money.' I cross my arms.

He raises a brow. 'Your money hey. I believe it was given to me by Dawson, was it not? Compensation from someone attempting to pick-pocket me.'

I poke my tongue out at him and he shakes his head. 'Childish.'

We make our way towards the house and enter the once glorious abode.

The house would have been magnificent if maintained, featuring four rooms on the ground floor it appears to be made of grey stone. The thick wooden support beams still stand; despite most of the inside having crumbled.

Asherton hurries into a large open area with a magnificent staircase leading to a landing with floorboards missing; I cautiously follow. He turns left into a room with a vaulted ceiling and large, dirty bay windows. An ancient bed takes up the centre of the room and he hurries across the dusty emerald carpet towards a large black marble hearth.

Asherton tosses wood in the hearth from a basket near the base and pulls a box of matches from his pocket. He sets to lighting a fire while I sit on a wooden window seat and rub a pane free of grime with the sleeve of my shift and peer out into the extensive shadowy grounds.

I turn as his boots thud across the floor and stop a few feet away from me. 'So, do you want to know what the job is?'

I have drawn my knees up to my sore ribs and wince as I turn my head to stare at him. 'Yeah, I guess I don't have a choice.'

'You could always go back.'

'And be beat up or worse?'

Asherton shrugs. 'Still a choice.'

'Hey, is this your house?' I yawn, exhaustion flooding every inch of my tired and aching body.

He sighs. 'Yeah. I'm a very broke lord. I usually stay in my room at the inn and live off a meagre monthly stipend my father left me before dying in the war. My mother died having me and I retained some of her jewels upon inheriting this place. It's seen better days. When the fighting entered the outskirts of Shaol my home took collateral damage. My father took me to town; I was six at the time. He returned to defend our home and lost his life.'

'I am sorry for your loss, but how are you going to pay me then?'

'Well, the job pays eleven coins which totals the rest of your fine and it will be paid with your freedom after you help me retrieve an item.' He sits down on the seat next to me. 'I'll sweeten the deal.' He slides a silver ring with a red stone from his left index finger and tosses it towards me. 'You can keep that too. It was my mother's.' He rubs his chin, lost in thought. 'How bad are you hurt?'

I slide my knees to the floor and resist the urge to wince. 'Haven't checked.'

'Well, I'll leave the room and you can do so. Call me when you are done.' He stands and hurries past the fire; a log cracks, sparks rising into the air as he exits into the hallway.

I scramble to my feet, pocket the ring and stare at the latch on the window. I wince as I stand on the seat, lean over and unlatch it. Pulling up my shift and wedging it in to my under things, I slide my now bare legs out the window and hurry through, landing with a soft crunch in the gravel. I stay close to the outer wall and run towards the road. I can have this ring appraised, sell it and, with the proceeds, make my way towards the capital. I will never be beholden to another.

'Rue.' Asherton's muffled voice calls out my name in the distance as I sprint towards the road.

Guilt washes over me and I hesitate; the lapse makes me lose my advantage and he sprints towards me through the front door, his fists clenched, his eyes narrowing on me. 'After I rescued you.'

I reach into my pocket and toss the ring at him; he catches it, my guilt disappears and I turn on my heel and run. Elation floods my body and I smile as I race down the road towards town. If I am caught he will likely have me thrown back in prison.

Coming to a halt, my body is enlivened by the exercise and my spirit soars. I laugh, the sound almost intrusive and in contrast to the softer sounds of evening. I wander over to a fallen log and plop down on to it, drawing my shift from my undergarments. Well, I have no food, no boots or money. How am I going to get out of this? My mother despises me so there is no way she will let me stay with her.

A branch snaps nearby and I glance up. Asherton glares at me before he steps forward and wraps a blanket around my shoulders. 'That was stupid. You have even less than me and ran away injured in the dark with no food or money.'

My eyes widen. I stole this man's things, ran from him yet he still was thoughtful enough to bring me a blanket. He reaches for my hand and places the ring in it. 'Take it.

My father always helped others. Just, when you are better off, return the favour.'

He stands and turns back towards his home. As the sound of his boots thudding on the dirt path fade into the distance I hesitate, wriggling my toes idly in the sand off the side of the track, an activity that always helps me think.

What have I got to lose? I hurry back towards the manor, vacillating in the entrance for a time before entering his bedroom. It feels like an hour has passed; the fire has been banked down and Asherton tosses and turns under his bedcovers. His robes and belt hang off a hook next to the fireplace and I brush my hand down the warm garments. My nostrils flare and a familiar scent makes my heart quicken. I jerk my hand back as if I had been burned.

I wander over to the window seat and lie down, drawing the blanket around me.

'You came back.'

The sudden words cause me to startle out of my slumber and jump, falling onto the ground tangled in the blanket.

Asherton laughs and I humph as I disengage myself from my fluffy foe. As I turn to stare at him my cheeks heat; my gawd, he is a fine specimen. Standing over me, dressed only in britches, his calves are a work of art. My eyes ascend slowly, taking in his chiselled abs, the golden curls on his chest, those muscular arms and I release my breath slowly, appreciating his form like he is a magnificent sculpture.

'My eyes are up here.'

My gaze meets his and I look away at the smug expression I find there. 'What exactly do you do for a living?'

He shifts his feet and hurries over to stoke the fire with a poker. 'Matters little.'

I stand up and wander over to his bed and sit on the edge. 'If we are to work together shouldn't I know a little bit about my employer?'

He scoffs and turns towards me. 'You want information from me yet I know nothing about you.'

I bite my lip, pondering what to give to have him trust me. 'My first name isn't Rue, it's Ervina.'

He steps towards me and warmth floods through me. 'Pretty. Now, I need you to steal a magic item for me in the capital. I had a betrothal contract with a noble woman stationed there. She backed out of the contract when her father thought I wasn't good enough.' He grits his teeth. 'He assumed I was a cad. Rumours caused by idle gossip I assure you, and I want revenge for the loss of my reputation. She has hair like yours so we may be able to get away with it.'

'I thought the Velshere are despised.'

Asherton rolls his eyes. 'Only in these backwaters. In Valdarn they are treated as any fae and in Still Waters are put to work for the benefit of the populace if introduced properly and without a criminal record. My mother was fae.'

My brows knit together. 'How are you not Velshere?'

He shrugs. 'Sometimes it happens, often it doesn't. But I inherited her ability to talk with fae creatures like that Bagere you met yesterday. His name is Guts and he loves his food.'

'Did your dad teach you the fae tongue?'

He nods, closing the gap between us. 'Tell me about yourself.'

'I sigh. My fae father was a wandering troubadour named Rueford who seduced my mother Liza Owens. I was the result. She hated me and raised me with little affection and sent me to school in town fifteen years ago. I learnt to do basic stuff and failed the other subjects, taking to the streets at eighteen. I fell in with a pack of other ne'er-do-wells and the rest is history.'

'Do you remember the war?'

'Snippets. I was three when it occurred.'

'So, your sick mother, was that a lie?'

I shake my head. 'A year ago I went back and found her ill. I stayed a few days until she started on me again then I fled. I drop in occasionally with medication but don't stay. You know, I've never really told anyone this before.'

Asherton reaches for my arm and frowns. 'You will have a bruise here.'

'My ribs are the worst.'

'I'd ask to take a look but that would be too forward.'

I splutter. 'Why would you need to look?'

He hurries over to his robes and dons them before he reaches into his pouch and retrieves a small book of spells. 'As you know, I can speak Valdarnish. I know a little magic. Most spells are written in that tongue which I can also read.'

I smile. 'Impressive, magic is rare.'

He shrugs. 'Less so amongst those who are related to fae. My father wanted me to be a sorcerer. I started arcane school at five. But after he died they kicked me out and this book is all I have left from those days. Will you let me take a look?'

I begin to remove my shift, struggling as I lift it over my head, and roll on to my side, my back towards him so even my chest band is mostly covered.

I am tempted to jump as he places his warm hand on my side. 'They really messed you up, you probably broke a couple of ribs.'

Paper rustles and I snuggle down amongst the bedding. Yawning, I close my eyes. His hand brushes a rib; my breath catches in my throat. It isn't fear that floods throughout my body, and I bite my lip. *No, Ervina, you do not want his hands to caress your back, don't imagine what it would be like for them to spread oil all over you and massage the tension out of your sore body.*

'*Ish ver dah bah den are.*' His hand warms and relief floods through my sore body. 'I reckon that will help.'

I nod. 'Sure.'

As he moves away from me I turn, my eyes flickering open as he tosses the book on the bed and slides under the covers.

'What are you doing?'

'I'm tired and we both need to be well-rested in the morning. This is my bed and I am not going to kiss my employee. That would be unprofessional.'

'I never even mentioned that.' I give him a cold stare.

He rolls over in the opposite direction. 'Night. Not that I am opposed to kissing beautiful women such as yourself.'

'I'll not share a bed with a flirty noble unless there is no other option.' I clamber out of the bed and pad over to the window.

'I'll take note of that,' he calls out.

I scowl in the direction of the bed, wrap myself in the blanket and perch on the window seat as sleep eludes me.

Chapter Five

I yawn, my chin resting on my knees as I stare out the grimy window. Sunlight filters in through the patch I cleared last night and warms my face. My body is weary as the sun rises. Always the night owl, I am at my fittest when the moon is visible in the sky. Something my mother often belittled me about; "that damn demon child never sleeps," she would cry. Come morning she would set me to chores but often found me snoozing amongst the chickens or rosemary bushes in our tiny backyard.

Drawing the blanket closer around me, I cock my head in the direction of the bed as Asherton throws back the covers and blinks in the morning light. His mop of blond curls falls over his eyes and he brushes them away. There is an unfamiliar tightness in my chest; if only I could run my hand through those curls. My stomach gurgles and he grins at me before turning his legs outwards and shoving his big feet into his boots. He stands, tousles his hair and grins at me before he strides past me out of the room. Can he read minds?

Standing up, I drape the blanket across my shoulders and wander towards the hallway. I stare in the direction of the stairs which creak under the weight of my host's heavy footfalls. My heart leaps into my throat as a plank snaps and his foot crashes through. His knuckles are white as they grip the balustrade.

'What are you doing?'

He turns his head towards me. 'Getting you some things that you need.'

The stair creaks as he ascends and I hold my breath, bolting towards the stairwell as he slips and bangs his knee before he leaps over the top broken stair and lands inelegantly on the upper deck. I release my held breath and gulp in the sweet air of relief as he wanders through a shattered doorway. The timbers of the doorframe look ready to crumble under the weight of the cracked ceiling.

He drags a trunk out of the room and halts, before dipping his finger in the dust and drawing a pattern. I cover my smile with my hand on my mouth. 'Hey Ma and Pa. I'm sure you won't mind; I have a friend in need.'

He proceeds to walk backwards, dragging his large burden, halting at the top of the stairs. His eyes narrow on the gap and he sighs. 'I need your help.'

I take the stairs two at a time, the challenge of little consequence to my smaller and more dexterous form. Stopping just before the gap, I stare at the love heart he has traced in the chest's surface and my heart softens; *just a little*, I staunchly tell myself.

'I can't take this down the stairs on my own in these robes.'

'True enough.'

Asherton grabs the handle of the chest in front of him. 'We will lift it over this gap and I will call out directions so you don't fall.'

I reach for the opposite handle and we lift in tandem.

'Careful, one step down, gentle.' He steps over the gap as I reach a step lower. 'Again, same depth but step towards the right as the wood is weaker on the left.

'Ok.' I follow his directions, and we continue our descent. Halfway down the tall staircase he skids on his robes. I falter, my leg slipping through the gap his foot had. I clutch my burden, refusing to drop the cumbersome, yet obviously sentimental thing, and glance up as sweat beads on my brow. With a thud, my employer drops his end and the chest lurches forward. I pull and lean back as he jumps onto the step beside me and unwraps my hands from the trunk. It wedges itself into the gap and entraps my leg.

Asherton is suddenly pressed up against me. His strong hand wraps around my right ankle as he attempts to unpin me, but my foot is fully entrapped. He kicks at the wood beneath us and it cracks. The sound is deafening as the chest topples forward and he leaps to the step below me.

He is quick for a man his size as his arms wrap around my middle, pulling me towards him, safe in his grasp.

Our breaths are ragged and he gives me a cold, hard stare. 'Do not put yourself in danger like that again.'

'That obviously meant something to you.'

I stare up at him and his eyes darken. 'Oh it does. I have yet to understand how and why it happened so quickly.'

My brows knit in confusion. 'Is there a double meaning behind those words?

He pulls me closer, his hand slipping to the curve of my hip. 'Do you want it to?'

I push myself off him, turn on my heel and make my way back to the ground floor. My heart hammers in my chest as confusion washes over me. I don't have time for this flirtatious nonsense. I have had a few relationships but none have ever worked out. The men I chose always left me after entering my bed, resulting in me never hearing from them again. Nobles, even the poorer ones, do not pursue common folk in the hope of marriage. This is a mess well avoided, no matter how kind and comely the man.

I turn and watch Asherton hurry over to the trunk; the lid has sprung open and emptied some of the contents on to the floor. 'Please go to the other room while I change.'

I shrug and pad across the hallway into the other room. A few minutes pass before he enters the room and hurries over to the bed. He cuts a dashing figure, having changed into trousers, a tailor-made red silk shirt, woollen cloak with hood, and blue leather riding boots.

He places a green kirtle, black silk shoes with a decent heel and silver buckles, stockings and a warm brown velvet shawl on the bed before me like some great offering. 'You will have to dress the part.' He sighs. 'If you are to act like my fiancée you best know my name. 'I am Lord Willaford Bexley Asherton the Fifth of Fishluck Hall. My father called me Will, my friends used Ash, which I would prefer as it lends authenticity to our ruse. The capital screens the purpose of all newcomers. Those of fae descent are scrutinized more thoroughly.'

'Interesting name.' I grin.

He rolls his eyes and gestures to the clothes. 'They were my mother's. They may be a little big on you.' He stares at my chest.

'I will take extra care of the clothes. Now leave so I can change.'

He ambles out of the room and stands whistling in the hall as I dress. As I finish, I exit the room. 'Tie me up, please.'

His eyes bug in his head. 'In what context?'

'Flirty scoundrel.' I glare at him. 'The laces on the dress.'

He shrugs and I turn away as he begins to lace me up, tightening the stays around my bosom, causing them to become a prominent feature of my outfit. 'You fill the gown out just fine.'

I am tempted to slap him, then remember most women wear their gowns thus, and draw the shawl up over my shoulders. 'What next?'

'We best make haste; it is two days east from here by foot to Silver Waters.' He pulls a dagger from his pocket and hands it to me; I slip it into my boot.

'I'm hungry.' I turn to face him.

He chuckles. 'Ah yes, your stomach made mention of that a time ago. There is an orchard on the way and often has traders selling foodstuffs.'

He heads to the overturned trunk and turns it upright before rummaging around inside. He withdraws a small purse and ties it to his belt and slips a scroll into the pocket of his pants before closing the lid of the chest. 'Thanks Ma and Pa for always looking out for me.'

Ash steps past me and hurries outside. I follow, catching up to his quick pace, and walk beside him. It is a beautiful day with a clear skies and birds whistling amongst the scattered and infrequent flowering plants. More common plants include aloe and lavender whose roots could find purchase in the sandy dunes either side of us. Our journey is made easier by the cobblestone road; other people wander by, a few heading towards the capital and others in the direction of Shaol. Some commoners are pushing hand-carts while others carry tools such as scythes and pickaxes.

Several people dip their hats or stop to gossip about the weather with Ash. He hurries along, soon lost in thought.

'You ok?'

Ash nods. 'Worried about this venture and also I need a pet name for you.'

'Why?'

'He shrugs. 'Why not?'

I sigh. 'Fine, do your worst.'

'Vi.'

'Not too shabby.'

Ash steps off the road a little into our journey and passes through an archway fenced either side with wicker panelling. A woman seated behind a rough wooden table near the entrance smiles at us in greeting. In the distance several people climb the palm trees or are picking dates or beach plums; half the trees offer very little or are sickly looking.

'Take your pick.' Ash smiles and gestures to the woven baskets on the table.

Never have I had someone offer to pay for a meal, other than my mother, and a strange sensation settles within. I hurry forward, my hand hovering over the juiciest fruits imaginable. I approach the situation with a sense of decorum, this man is generous, not rich and I should hold back. I pluck out two dates and a few plums.

He picks out two coconuts and a plum before placing four coins in the woman's hands. 'Thank you.'

'Sir, this is too much.' The older woman stares at the coins in her hands.

I begin chewing on a date.

'Keep it, madam. Food is scarce and your trees need care.' Ash begins eating the plum and wanders back the way we came. I follow close on his heels.

He stops and waits and I slam into his back. Turning, he leans over me, his hand dips into his pocket and he pulls out a handkerchief and dabs it across my lips. 'Better.'

'What was that?'

My cheeks burn and he smiles smugly. 'Cute.'

I grumble to myself and he chuckles as we exit the orchard. The journey soon becomes monotonous a few hours in and we stop on the side of the road. A woman with a bucket and ladle is selling water. Ash reaches into the bucket and lifts the ladle to my lips. Parched, I slurp down the water with little care of how greedy I look.

'One coin a ladle.' The vendor holds out her palm.

I almost choke on my drink. 'Expensive for something that should be free.'

The water seller shrugs her shoulders. 'You know rain is scarce and I bet you are unlikely skilled enough to try divining for fresh water. It is hardly found in abundance for wells to be dug. My family are water diviners, a skill handed down from my ma and her ma. We all have to work somehow to make a living.'

I cross my arms. Why do people need to tell me their life story when I make a statement? Less words and more action is a creed I live by.

Ash pulls out a coin and his brow wrinkles as he drops it into the woman's outstretched palm. 'Not much left I'm afraid.'

Strangely enough I can handle this man's excessive use of words, his statement doesn't grate on my nerves. Never one for company, Ash's presence is strangely comforting. The thought makes me feel uneasy and my fingers tense and I halt my drinking.

Ash motions for me to hurry but I lift the ladle to his lips. He brushes it aside; his brows rise as I glower and he allows me to offer him a drink. As he swallows, his eyes fill with gratitude I have not earned; he is the one paying.

'You are scary when you look at me like that.'

I give him a smug smile and he laughs. 'Confident ladies are very attractive.'

'Stop saying stuff like that. I am no lady.' I playfully push him away.

We continue our journey until the sun is above our heads, its blazing heat causing us to sweat profusely, so much so that we have shed our cloaks and carry them in our arms.

'Too hot to continue.' Ash wipes his brow with his sleeve before striding to the side of the road and spreading his cloak on a sandy dune, plopping down onto it. I do the same.

Ash takes out a dagger and uses it to cut a hole in the two coconuts. He hands me one and we drink the contents before he cracks them open on a rock and we scoop out the meat.

'This is our last meal of the day. I am sorry. I need to save what I have for tomorrow.'

I shrug. 'I have often had less in a day.'

Ash's eyes fill with anger. 'Well, I'll see to it that you eat well from now on. Get some meat on your bones.'

'You sound like some evil creature trying to fatten me up for dinner.' I chuckle.

'Oh I can imagine you with curves.' The lazy smile he gives me next makes my heart quicken. 'But you will eat as you need your strength.'

'It's not like you can do anything about it once I have completed the job and we part company.'

'Don't be too sure about that, Vi.'

I swear I can almost hear anger in his voice and I stare at him; his words almost sound possessive. Ash concentrates on removing his boots, oblivious to my gaze. The warmth and pleasant company has a soothing effect on me and I lie back as the slight breeze, laced with the scent of flowers and the saltiness of the sea, caresses my face.

'I could go for a dip right now.'

The urge to run wild and shed my hefty outer layers courses through me and I give him a bemused smile as he leans over me.

'What is so funny?'

He reaches out and brushes a tendril of my vibrant blue hair out of my face and his eyes lock on my mouth.

'I was laughing at my outrageous thoughts.'

'We all have those.' He sits upright. 'Time to go I reckon.'

We stand and retrieve our cloaks and make haste to continue our journey.

*

Ash marches off the road towards a coppice of stunted trees and throws down his cloak, this last hour he has been unsettled, like his emotions are churning within. He paces amongst the trees before I sit cross-legged at the base of one.

'Are we stopping for the night?' I ask.

'Yes.'

'I'm exhausted.' I lean against the trunk.

'I'll take the first watch, you take the second,' he mutters.

I turn to stare at him. 'What's wrong?'

He shrugs. 'An itch I can't scratch. It truly is unrighteous of me to even foster the thought of it.'

'I'm a thief. Righteousness is hardly my forte.'

Ash laughs suddenly. 'True enough.'

'I'm willing to allow you to offload your secrets on me.'

He gives me a quizzical look. 'I doubt it.'

'Try me.'

He shrugs and kneels in front of me. I gasp as he grips my chin with his right hand, his eyes are vivid pools of emotion. Ash lowers his face inches from mine. I gulp; that movement makes his pupils dilate, then his mouth is on mine. He drags his teeth across my upper lip, forcing my mouth to yield. His other hand pushes the back of my head, dragging me closer and allowing him deeper access. The kiss is possessive, his tongue is skilled and my body is soon hot with longing.

Ash draws away, his hands dropping to his sides, his eyes smoulder with intensity. 'One intrusive thought dealt with. By the gods, it was worth it.'

'What the hell!'

Before I can even gather my thoughts he has pulled away, launched himself to his feet and hurried two trees over to lean his back against a trunk. 'Get some sleep. I will wake you in a few hours.'

Trembling, I roll over on my side and squeeze my eyes shut. Confusion and exhaustion vie for equal control and I give in too easily to the latter as I am not ready to confront my befuddlement. I hadn't hated him kissing me, almost as if it was the most natural thing in the world. But so is sleep and I need that more as of this moment.

Chapter Six

Ash's watch has ended and mine has begun. After an hour of staring at the road I lie back, staring up at the night sky. The moon is no longer full but still shows herself reluctantly and keeps me company. I have always loved the Valdarnian story of the moon fae Dornian and her human lover.

The fable tells of a time when there were no stars in the sky and only the moon for light. The lonely moon maiden fell for a young shepherd watching over his flock of sheep at dusk; a gentle soul who always gave thanks to the moon for her light.

The shepherd was kind and even reluctant to kill predators. Dornian gifted him with magic via a Salvane crystal, Salvane being the Valdarnian word for magic. It is the only word I cared to ask my mother about when I was ten.

Delighted with his newfound skill, the shepherd used magic to illuminate the night. No longer in need of Dornian's light, he soon forgot her existence. The moon goddess became distressed, leaving the sky and abandoning wayfarers who relied on her light to their fates so she could seek out the man she loved.

A bird cries out in the dark; I sit up and stare at the road. A pair of gleaming eyes lock on mine. A branch snaps and causes a grey wild dog to turn and bolt away from our camp and scurry out of sight over the dunes. I shrug and return to my pondering.

Dornian's story is not a happy one but a tragic tale of two vastly different lovers. It is much like my own romantic history except without the magic. The two fell in love but Dornian steals the crystal which causes the shepherd to curse her name and banish her to the heavens, bound to be forever lonely yet forced to give light to all even though they no longer praised her.

It is written that the curse can only be broken when the moon maiden dons a mortal shell living the life of a thief, destined to steal until her beloved is reborn and gives up power or his life for her. Only then will she remember who she is and find happiness.

A low growl behind me causes me to stiffen, the hairs on my neck rising like hackles on a rabid wolf. I turn slowly as a giant, black-feathered beast towers over me. Its large maw is open wide, yellowed teeth glint in the moonlight as warm drool drips from its mouth onto my face. I roll out of the way as the strange creature's piglike snout crashes into the earth.

It howls, a strange noise interrupted with chirps and snuffling, appropriate for the odd hybrid of ostrich, wolf and boar. Ash leaps to his feet and draws the book from his pocket as I dodge around the creature; it bolts towards me flapping its wings.

Its long neck whips towards me and it bares its teeth and stares at me; its eyes are glimmering pools of rage. Trembling, I slide the dagger from my boot and sidestep out of the way as its claws slam into the earth where I was. My heart hammers in my chest, sweat pours off me as I twist away from the beast, dodging a bite and swerving left, missing a deadly slash from a raking claw.

I duck under the beast and roll aside before I leap to my feet and charge the monster. The knife glitters in the dark, almost as if it has captured the light from the heavens. The creature looks past me and doesn't move as I ram my dagger into his hindquarters. It screeches before rounding on me and pouncing. My back crashes into sand, my arm pinioned under a large claw. The dagger slides out of my hand as my enemy lowers its maw towards me, its rancid breath steaming in the night air.

Ash slams into its side with his shoulder; the beast grunts and turns. With my arm now free, I leap to my feet and bolt for the trees. The need to survive courses through my veins, before I stop, remembering my friend. Sighing, I turn and bolt towards Ash.

Ash holds out his book, his hands glow blue. '*Forta festoon, naveria.*'

The beast snorts and rushes him, halting inches before him, dancing restlessly on the spot.

'*Forta festoon.*' Ash's brows knit in concentration. He holds out his hand towards the beast as it lowers its gleaming fangs.

Fear surges through me, pushing me to action. I run, ducking briefly to snatch up the dagger. I glow momentarily as the light floods through me. Warming me, it removes my fear. I am a blur, invisible to both friend and foe, and I raise my weapon, plunging it into the foreleg of the monster.

The creature howls and leaps in my direction, its eyes wild with confusion. I do not have time to dodge before Ash hurtles towards the beast unknowingly giving me enough wiggle room to slide to the left and out of danger.

The creature's claw slices through Ash's right leg; he cries out in pain and lands on his backside as the beast looms over him. Blood trickles from an angry gash on his leg. 'Where are you, Vi? I must save her. *Duska Uniderris.*'

I turn at the sound of whinnying. A unicorn rears up in the air, its hooves striking outwards; its golden shaggy coat catches the starlight. Then it canters towards our foe. The monster and the horse of light square off. The strange hybrid roars and the unicorn knickers and tosses its mane as if it is dismissing the monster as a mere annoyance.

'Please take her away from here. I know a unicorn can see through any spell.' Ash reaches towards the golden horse as it rushes past him. 'No!'

The unicorn rams its horn into our foe. The strange creature howls before turning and bolting towards the east. The unicorn trots over to Ash and butts his head with its nose. My hands begin to glow with moonlight; the magic spreads over me and my whole body glows. I turn to stare at my friend.

Ash's eyes widen. 'No, it can't be.' He reaches for my hand and abruptly snatches it back like I am a curse ready to undo him.

'I guess you can see me now.'

'Yes.'

'Thank you for saving me.'

He nods and takes out his magic book. Flipping through the pages, his hands glow with green light and the wound begins to knit itself together. '*Clottin Morte.*'

I step towards him as he stands and mounts the unicorn. 'He will get us there faster.'

I try to climb up but am awkward as I have never ridden before. My employer reaches down and pulls me up. He snatches his hand back like I am some plague-infested being as I settle in for the ride. The unicorn trots towards the main road.

'We will ride until twilight tomorrow. I am not risking you to danger again.'

'Can the unicorn take that?'

'We will stop briefly, but yes.'

I lean against him; his chest is warm against my back. His heart beats quicker before his arms encircle me and he leans forward, his unshaved face rough against my ear. 'Who are you?'

'Elvina Owens. You already have my given name.'

'Are you sure?' He groans. 'That Orwolf did a number on my leg. Not bleeding but still painful.'

'Is that what that monster is called?'

He straightens and the absence of his nearness and want of it shocks me.

'Yep.'

'How did you call the unicorn?'

He shifts and I am jolted, his strong calves pressing against mine. 'First spell I learnt. I didn't get expelled from school for my lack of parentage.'

The sun rises above the horizon as dawn approaches.

'What then?'

'I couldn't master beyond basic cantrips. My ex-fiancée promised me a Salvane crystal when we wed. When she backed out I was denied it. I want you to steal it for me in the hopes I can master more complex spells.'

'Aren't they dangerous?' I shiver and his arms wrap around me.

'Well, you can become invisible now, can't you? My little moon maiden.'

I giggle. 'What a ridiculous notion.'

'I wouldn't be so sure.'

The rest of the day is long and the trip arduous. The dawn gives way to noon and the heat of our close bodies becomes unbearable. My nostrils flare, now truly aware of how bad I must smell.

We stop just after midday near a well and drink our fill. I wash my face, hands and neck. My companion strips off his shirt and washes to the waist as I wander amongst the nearby shrubs. I smile as my eyes alight on a strawberry patch. I hurry back to Ash, who has dressed himself, and gesture for him to follow.

He hurries after me and smiles broadly. 'Well, that's a wonderful sight.'

We pick and consume the berries ravenously, the sweet juice coating both our lips.

'That shade suits you.' I gesture to his mouth.

Ash grins. 'You as well.'

'I want to learn Valdarnish.'

'I can help you with that.'

I pick another berry. 'What does that phrase *Remarda Cevere* mean?'

Spots of colour blossom on his cheeks. '*Remarda* means come. *Cevere* means sweetheart or it's a term of endearment for a beloved partner depending on the tone and body language. Valdarnish relies on inflection and fluid gestures and less words than human Rersherish.'

'Oh … but I am neither to you.' I glance away.

'Don't worry about it too much, remember I called Guts that too.'

'Oh, so I am your pet now.' I scowl in his direction.

His purse chitters and those strange eyes peer up at me.

'Guts sees himself as a friend rather than a pet.' He plucks a strawberry and holds it above the Bagere who opens its budlike mouth. The strawberry is sucked within to the sound of vigorous chomping.

'Is reading body language a skill you use to seem like you are reading my mind?'

He chortles and the sound is like magic. 'Yes.'

I don't know what comes over me as I hold a strawberry to Ash's mouth. His eyes narrow on mine and he opens his lips; his breath is warm on my fingers. 'Maybe I'm *your* pet.'

I laugh, trying to break the obvious friction between us. 'What are we doing?'

He shrugs. 'Some would say falling in love.'

I back away from him. 'Don't be ridiculous.'

His eyes darken and he turns on his heel. We wander away from each other to complete the call of nature before washing our faces and hands again at the well and indulging in another long drink each before Ash lifts me onto the unicorn.

He takes a bucket from the well and offers it to the majestic beast. As the unicorn drinks its fill, Ash stares up at me, his jaw tense. The unicorn paws the ground impatiently and my employer pulls himself up onto our mount.

I lean forward so my stomach almost touches the unicorn's neck.

'Don't be ridiculous,' he grunts out before he settles me between his hard thighs. 'You can't ride like that.'

We do not speak for the rest of the journey to the capital. The tension between us in the awkward silence is almost palpable.

Chapter Seven

The unicorn slows and stops atop a sandy dune; the view is a sight to behold. Silver water glows in the moonlight, flowing swiftly under a magnificent golden wooden bridge. Guards in similar uniform to those in Shaol wander up and down carrying lanterns, sometimes halting near a huge portcullis set into a gargantuan stone wall. To the left of the bridge, the cobblestone road ends in a cul-de-sac with three large, wooden buildings with tiled roofs. A silk pennant flutters in the breeze; the universal sign in Rersherdia for inn.

Ash leans back as I dismount before he slides off the steed, talking gently to the unicorn in what I assume is Valdarnian before he pets it gently on the muzzle. The beautiful beast turns around and bolts away. Ash winces before limping down the dune towards the inn, his back to me. I hurry towards him, bracing myself into his side to support his downward journey.

'Don't touch me.' He stops and turns to stare at me.

I take a step back, my eyes narrowing on his. 'What have I done?'

His eyes soften. 'There is a distant memory that fills me with shame. I took a gift and misused it.'

I shrug. 'We all have regrets.'

'You don't understand.' His jaw clenches. 'When I witnessed your power it brought back an ancient memory of us.'

My brows rise in puzzlement. 'We only met a few days ago.'

He sighs. 'Yes and no.'

'Very vague.'

He begins to meander towards the inn. 'Let's get some rest, we have a big day tomorrow.'

His shoulders droop wearily and, in a hasty decision to cheer him, I sneak up on him. I become invisible, slip my hand into his pocket and remove something small and warm. I will hand over the stolen goods after I buy him a drink, and I giggle as I remove my gift of invisibility.

We reach the inn; the sound of revelry greets us, the night no longer peaceful as Ash pulls open the door. We enter the first floor; the room is hazy with smoke from cigars and reeks of sweat and stale ale. The space is well-lit by candles placed on the bar and tables. Patrons clink glasses and the roar of loud conversation is deafening.

Ash hurries over to the bar and I follow. 'Two ales, please.' He fumbles in his pocket.

The barkeep, a large and dour looking man, hands over the tin mugs, sloshing the contents on the bar.

'Do you have a room available?' Ash asks.

The bartender nods. 'Yeah, a singleton.'

'We will take it.' My companion turns and grins at me. 'I'm done in. But I guess you have to share with a flirty noble now there are no other options.'

The barkeep clears his throat. 'One coin for the ale, four for the room.'

Ash turns back to the other man and pulls his empty hand from his pocket. He glances about before he answers through gritted teeth. 'I think I have been robbed.'

The barkeep nods to a man in the corner dressed in a shabby grey cloak who hurries towards my employer.

'Hey, wait, I'm usually good for this.' Ash slides off the stool, his hands up in supplication. 'Let me talk to my friend.'

I hurry between him and his would-be captor and drop Guts on to the counter. 'I'll cover his drinks and book the room.' Unsure of what to do next, I wing it. I tickle the Bagere's back, receiving strange looks from the bartender and nearby patrons.

I glance to Ash, he sighs. 'I should have suspected you from the start, but I thought I could trust you. Tell him how many coins you need.'

'Six, Guts.' The creature chitters and coins clink and drop onto the counter from its little mouth. I slide the coins towards the bartender.

The bartender scowls and snatches up the coins. 'Fair enough, but this fellow is out of here.'

Guts chitters; the bartender's mouth hangs open as the little creature sprouts legs, scampers across the bar and launches itself, landing on Ash's shoulder who levels a glare at me. 'We will talk about this later.'

The grey-cloaked man grabs Ash by his collar and all but throws him out of the bar to peals of laughter. Ash dusts off his clothes and holds his head high as he wanders off.

'What are the other buildings?' I face the bartender as he hands me a key.

'Stable and post office.' The bartender turns to serve another as I hurry up a set of stairs to the left of the bar.

When I enter my room I give into laughter before guilt racks my insides. I undress down to my shift and lie on the bed as sleep eludes me. Surely Ash will return to confront me?

The noise from the floor below lessens and, without constant action to keep me from having to process the day, a sudden realisation sweeps through me. My heart betrays me as my mind tries to deny the feeling Ash's presence invokes in me. Security, friendship, desire and another niggling one I refuse to entertain.

I need to get him out of my system and there is only one sure fire way to do so. I wait a little longer and, when the inn is almost silent, I hurry down the set of stairs and out the front door. What if he has left? Anxiety clutches my insides. Hastening my steps, I hurry around the back of the building. No trace of him, just a drunk woman vomiting in a shrub.

'Hey, did a young man with blond hair pass this way?'

She nods and points to the other buildings. 'Wandered into one of those about twenty minutes ago.'

My hands begin to glow and the woman stumbles backwards before fleeing, her face a mask of fear. A tug, like a rope attached to my navel draws me towards a barnlike structure. The smell of manure and nickering of horses identifies the building as the stables.

I stand in the open doorway as Ash lies prone, tossing and turning amongst the hay-strewn floor. A horse nearby stomps around in its stall and the man before me covers his ears.

'Quiet, you rascal.'

I quell the urge to giggle, his terseness a façade I know well, and pad over to the man that had saved my life. The man that has given me a sense of security and friendship without demanding something in return. The hay is prickly and dry under my bare feet.

'Ash.' Since these feelings have awoken, his name is like honey on my tongue, like a promise of things to come.

He rolls over in the hay and my mind turns to naughtier things. His brows rise in a quizzical expression. 'Why are you here? You took the last of my money and my chance at a good night's rest. I was humiliated.'

I kneel before him and his eyes narrow, annoyance replaced with something almost feral as his gaze sweeps over the sheer shift I am wearing void of undergarments.

He gulps and glances away. 'What do you want, Vi? I'm in no mood to be pleasant company.'

My shortened name in that strong thick accent almost undoes my courage. I hold out a hand and he stares as if it is some traitorous double-edged blade. 'I am sorry for stealing from you. I was just being playful. Join me, *Cevere.*'

His eyes soften at the sentiment. 'You are forgiven, Vi. But I am an honest man. If I follow you upstairs, I will kiss you and will be hard pressed to stop. I have designs on your body, your heart and if I could, your soul. Turn around and go back to bed if you cannot face that.'

A giddy thrill bursts within my core, and I lean forward and press a questing kiss to his mouth; his lips yield to mine.

'You should stop,' he whispers. The vibration against my lips builds my confidence and I devour his mouth with mine.

He pulls away, his breath ragged before he stands and draws me up against his chest. Hay cascades around us, sliding from his clothes. 'Are you inviting me to your bed?'

I nod enthusiastically and he grins, before snatching my hand in his, and hurries from the stables, pulling me almost savagely towards his urgent goal. His limp is still apparent but his obvious urgency overshadows that. My footfalls barely connect with the earth before we are inside the main building and our feet thud up the stairs.

We reach the room; Asherton throws open the door and pushes me towards the centre before he slams the door shut. I step backwards towards the single bed; his eyes are wild with need as he sheds his clothes. My eyes travel down his beautiful form, then I am in his arms and the night is ours.

Chapter Eight

I pace outside the inn, fully dressed, before the sun has even risen. I should be over him but last night has made it worse. He was such a conscientious and unselfish lover, something I have never experienced, and it has been my undoing. I couldn't face him this morning. This isn't worth it, this job isn't worth the feelings I have to endure. Yet I can't seem to leave.

'Vi.' Ash rushes through the front door of the inn, pulling his shirt over his head. His hair is dishevelled and his eyes filled with terror. 'Oh, there you are, *Cevere*.' He fixes his clothes and leans in to kiss me.

I put up a hand to stop him and he pulls away and frowns. 'What's wrong?'

'Last night is over. For what it is worth, I have no regrets but we are not together.'

He scowls. 'So that's it? Strictly business from now on?'

I nod. 'That's correct.'

'I see.' He turns on his heel and strides towards the bridge. 'Best to get a move on then, Rue.'

The lack of use of my real name is like a dagger to the heart but I can't blame him. Ash hurries across the bridge, his back is ramrod straight. He stops and turns, waiting for me to catch up. I give him a warm smile. His eyes widen and his hand brushes mine.

'There is something I need to get off my chest.' Ash sighs. 'It's about the job.'

A guard hurries towards us, blowing out his lantern as the sun rises behind us. 'Bit early to be entering the city.'

Ash's worried face is bathed in the morning sunlight as he turns his head to smile at the guard. 'We have had a long journey and would break our fast in one of the fine dining establishments in the city.'

The guard's brow furrows as he stares at me before he bows deeply. 'My lady.' He snaps upright and gestures to a sentry behind the portcullis. 'Open her up, Senior Lady Borcheston will want to see them at once.'

I purse my lips and stare at Ash. 'What is going on? That isn't me.'

The guard's hand hovers over the dagger hilt sheathed at his hip. 'Do you know this man, Lady Borcheston?'

My eyes rise to meet Ash's who mouths *yes*. My innards squirm, can I really trust my employer? I gulp as the guard's expectant gaze is locked on my mouth awaiting my answer. I freeze.

My companion reaches into his pocket and withdraws a rolled up scroll, which he hands to the guard who unfurls and reads it as the portcullis rises with the sound of crank-ing chains. Ash snatches up my hand and plasters a jovial smile on his lips as the guard hands back the scroll. 'Lady Borcheston and I can't wait to marry.'

'Everything appears to be in order, congratulations on your upcoming nuptials. I would recommend the Fae Wilds Tavern; the mixed grill is a delight.'

'Ash?' I try to pull my hand from my employer's grip.

He squeezes my hand and pulls me forward. 'We shall head there at once.'

We hurry through the portcullis; when we are some distance from the entrance to the city Ash draws me into a side street away from prying ears. He lifts my chin and his gaze drops to my mouth. My lips quiver and I choke back a sob. Uncertainty claws at my insides almost squeezing the air from my lungs.

'I haven't been entirely honest,' he mutters before he kisses me. His arms drop to my hips and pull me closer; his mouth roves over mine, claiming me. It is as if he is trying to reassure himself of my loyalty to his cause despite what he is soon to admit.

We pull away, gasping; my fists clench and I glare at him. 'Spit it out.'

He sighs and rubs the back of his head. 'I know your father.'

'What?' My hand leaps to my chest; my heart within beats unsteadily.

'In fact, it was your father who hired me for this job when your older sister Flynn returned my ring in public and denounced me as penniless and unworthy. I was a downtrodden noble who had hoped to work my way up but she saw to it I was humiliated. At twenty-six-years old, with the inhabitants of the city laughing at me, I sought refuge on the road.' Ash's eyes scan my face. 'Tell me you don't hate me, *Cevere*.'

I scowl. 'Hurry up.'

Ash smiles sadly. 'That is where I met your father, an ambassador disguised as a troubadour. Flynn was his daughter from an arranged marriage to a callous human noble, like so many matches that were made in hopes at preventing the war. Your father, Lord Rueford Regallion, took me under his wings and told me tales of a great love. He had been mutually separated from his wife for three years when he met his soulmate. When his love found out about his marriage she made him leave her and his beloved one-year-old daughter.'

I scoff and lurch forward, my hand ready to strike. 'You lie even now. My father was a troubadour who abandoned us.'

Ash snatches my hand and presses it to his chest above his heart. 'I expressed to him how I needed the Salvane crystal to focus my magical talent and sit the entrance exams for a scholarship to a magical college. I explained how his daughter Flynn had many suitors until they found out she was cold and mean like her mother. She only wanted power, reputation and looks in a partner. My family's name once held power and my father sacrificing his life for his family made me all the more desirable for the image of the husband with a heroic father.'

I clutch at his shirt, rage boiling within. 'Nobles always get what they want.'

His other hand begins to rub my back and I tense. 'I need to get away from you.'

Ash frowns. 'My father's heroic reputation would set tongues wagging in earnest and she would be in the limelight. I was a fool, I thought she cared for me and I asked after the crystal. Flynn toyed with me, half promising it to me if I wed her quickly, and so our betrothal contract was drawn up. I said we needed to get to know each other before marrying. She agreed until I disclosed to her that I was destitute and then she left me. After I relayed this to your father his face became grave and said he had left Flynn to her mother's care and wealth but wanted to bequeath his Valdarnish fortune to his youngest. Her name was Ervina Owens, and he gave me the last description he had of you some twenty years earlier when he had spotted you in Shaol with your mother.'

I struggle against Ash; he releases my hands. 'Your lie is getting out of hand.'

'Let me finish.'

'I think I have heard enough.' I turn on my heel and hurry away.

'Wait, Vi. He sent me to find you. He loves you.'

His boots thud on the slate tiles of the alleyway after me. My breath quickens as I bolt, my hair whips my face and stinging tears of pain and anger squeeze out of my half-closed eyes.

'Vi please!'

My blood pounds in my ears as he quickens his pace; his harsh breaths give away his closeness. I always thought I would arrive in Silver Waters filled with anticipation, not with my heart torn asunder. I focus on my newly awoken gift. Is it useable during the day? I concentrate, picturing a full moon and its light washing over me. Warmth spreads throughout me like I am on fire.

I stop and merge with the milling crowd and glance over my shoulder, Ash halts, his face is fearful, his eyes flittering about searching for me. Tears spill from his face and he brushes them away with the back of his hand. 'I was to deliver you safely into your father's care. I hired someone to track you down; I found out you were a thief. I played the mark for you; I was so sloppy and obvious that a career rogue would not be so easily fooled and forced into my bargain. I didn't expect to fall in love with you, Vi. Where are you?'

My breath shudders with the threat of my own tears and I turn away from him and lose myself amongst the masses.

Chapter Nine

Determined to make the best of my situation, I do what I always do in times of crisis, I shove my grievances down deep inside and give in to the physical pleasures of warmth, drink and delicious food. A magnificent city such as this is ripe for the picking and I soon find myself wandering amongst the thoroughfares of the well-planned city.

There are separate lanes for pedestrians and vendor carts which run vertical alongside roads for horse-drawn vehicles and infrastructure mainly built of sandstone. Smaller interconnecting paths lead directly to businesses and homes and it resembles a great web, almost as if built by a giant arachnid. The magnificent palace appears to be made of silver bricks and gleams in the distance like a wonderous beacon.

Gardens and orchards with trees almost stripped bare grace the outer parts of the city near the high walls. Here I wander, swilling wine from a leather skin and cramming hot pastries at interludes into my gullet, drowning my sorrows in the most ancient and usual of fashions. The vendors' carts are almost bare and most sell similar items including bread, coarse meat pies and fruit well past freshness. But at least the alcoholic beverages are readily available and incredibly cheap.

My purse is full and I chuckle. How will you eat tonight, Ash? Where will you sleep? My stomach lurches. Heck, what if he freezes or worse, gets robbed? It is ok if I rob him but no one else is allowed to pilfer his pockets. I grit my teeth. *Girl, you are trying to forget about him. You don't want his hot all-consuming kisses and you certainly don't want him whispering words of love in your ear as his breath caresses your neck.*

Hot tears fall from my eyes and I perch on a boulder near a small pond filled with fish; their rainbow scales glitter like the precious jewels secreted in my stolen purse. My eyes widen and my heart fills with joy. They are such magnificent creatures to behold. If only I had someone to express my joy to. I slip my hand into the lake and a curious fish nibbles my pinkie.

I waggle my finger and the creature dashes away. Crumbling some bread into the pond it soon writhes in a whirlpool of activity, the food disappearing into the bulging mouths of a variety of ravenous sea creatures swimming amongst the tempest.

That is how I feel right now, a small fish dashing away from the ferocious denizens of the ocean. At its centre is a beacon; one of burgeoning love, of need and want. But there are chinks in that beacon, built on a foundation of dishonesty from both of us. I sigh, knowing that I must find him even if we can't fix it. I still need closure. A bell tolls twice in the distance; it is around two hours after lunch and the day is passing by quickly.

Think, Ervina, where would Ash go to look for you? I roll my eyes, he probably thinks I am a terrible thief. So, he would likely hang out near a prison or other such affiliation. I stretch and push myself to my feet. Following the outer walls back the way I came, I cross a grassy parkland and merge with a crowd surging south towards the palace. I realise I am lost and have become flummoxed in the process. Genuinely disorientated I bump into a nobly dressed woman.

She is slightly older and as she rounds on me her mouth is set in a grim line. Her forehead wrinkles. 'A Velshere, I thought they were mere rumours.' Her cold calculating eyes roam my form. 'What is your name?'

'I am sorry, miss, for bumping into you.'

She shrugs. 'It matters little.'

I take in her appearance: brown eyes and blue hair like mine, how bizarre. 'I'm sorry, I didn't catch your name.'

She smirks. 'How ridiculous, everyone knows I am Lady Flynn of clan Regallion and house Borcheston.'

I bite my lip; this day is just getting more troublesome. 'I am truly sorry for my mistake. Could you tell me where the prison is?'

Flynn points towards the palace. 'It is in the eastern wing of that building. Are you looking for someone?'

A man dressed in a green shirt, britches, black boots and leather jerkin glowers at me; his face is craggier than hungry rats clawing through the earthen floor of a larder. He leans in to whisper to Lady Flynn. The noble woman hurries past me and tears a wanted poster from a dirty wall plastered with other faded fliers. She strides towards me and thrusts the paper outwards.

A simple illustration that faintly resembles my own image stares back at me with the words: *Reward wanted for information on the whereabouts of Ervina Owens* and a rough description of my looks and whereabouts.

Flynn clicks her fingers and her craggy-faced companion advances on me. I stumble backwards. The crowd splits and forms a circle around us and begins to hurl the regular insults my way.

'Untrustworthy Velshere.'

'Get the devil spawn off the street.'

I am done, there is nothing for me but hate here, even in a city as big as this, and I fall to my knees, the stress of it all consuming me.

'Get away from her.'

My head snaps up as Ash pushes people aside. Entering the inner circle, he plants himself between me and Flynn's companion.

'Lord Asherton, what brings you back to Silver Waters and even more handsome than before?' Flynn looks at him through lowered lids.

It is like a dagger has been jammed in between my ribs; jealousy bubbles out of a seeping wound and I rise to my feet. 'Ash?'

'You know this woman?' asks Flynn.

He turns and stares at me, his eyes softening. 'Do I?'

I hurl myself at him. 'Yes, you do.'

He loses his footing but manages to correct his stance before his arms encircle me.

'Twenty coins for those that can subdue these two,' Flynn shouts, her hands balled up in fists.

The crowd surges towards us. Ash shelters me in his arms, bellowing a couple of times as he is struck with anything the crowd can find. He droops and falls against me. Being a slight person, I stumble under his weight, the breath knocked from my body. Flynn's servant drags me away from Ash and tosses me over his shoulder. The crowd parts as Flynn steps towards them and chucks a handful of coins away from her. The mob acts like a flock of pigeons scrambling in the dust for a tidbit as they scramble to pick up the coins.

Ash groans but staggers to his feet. Flynn rushes to his side and supports him. His face is streaked with blood and his lip appears to be split. He leans heavily on the noblewoman and she almost drags him after us.

'Hush, my dear, I have you,' Flynn croons.

My captor turns and faces the palace, hurrying towards it. It is a matter of minutes before we reach it and I lift my head as we approach the majestic structure. It is not just a building but a work of art like a silver spiral horn from a unicorn. An ivory staircase winds its way up the tower and large stain glass windows are scattered throughout the design as well as a collection of emerald doors placed sporadically on various landings. Heck, it must be at least twelve storeys high.

We are met by a few guards who let us past with a brief bow to Flynn and we begin the climb. By the time we reach the sixth landing I feel like a sack of bruised potatoes. A sentry pulls open a door, we hurry through and I am tossed on the red carpeted ground. I grip my ribs as I fight against exhaustion, pain and budding hate for the power of the nobility. A woman having been kidnapped off the street while her friend was beaten and no one battering an eyelid at our mistreatment. Glenthon dumps me on the floor and smirks down at me as I glare at him.

Flynn guides Ash over to a comfortable chair and he drops into it. Leaning back, he closes his eyes. 'What do you want with us, Flynn?'

Flynn glowers at me before perching on the armrest and sweeping Ash's hair to one side. She traces a finger across his injured lip all while giving me an evil grin.

Ash stiffens and his eyes snap open and he slaps her hand away. 'This mouth is reserved for another, not one with a heart made of wood.'

Flynn sighs, slides to her feet and gracefully steps across the carpet towards a large wooden armoire. She throws open the doors and pulls out a gaudily painted box. Flynn rolls her hips playfully and saunters towards Ash as if he is some prey she will sink her hellish claws into.

Ash stares at her and laughs. 'What was that?'

Flynn glowers. 'It worked before.'

I hide my face in the carpet and groan. What happened between these two? Do I want to know? I have to get away from here, from this awkward conversation. I sit up and face the pair and try to formulate my escape.

Ash gives me a bemused smile. 'It never got beyond a couple of kisses, did it, Flynn?'

She shrugs. 'No, but it could.'

I glare at Ash. I burn with envy knowing how it feels to be kissed by him.

Ash laughs. 'Not like us, Vi.'

Flynn grinds her teeth. 'Shut up. I am talking.'

'What has your devious mind and shallow heart concocted?' Ash leans forward in the chair.

'Well, I have long had my fun. But it is time to settle down. Mama has all but cut me off if I don't wed soon.' She taps the box with long, perfectly painted nails. 'What your heart truly desires is in here.'

She opens the box, Ash's eyes almost bug out of his head and he shifts his gaze to mine before it flitters back to the prize set before him. 'What do you want from me?'

Flynn takes the jewel and the box drops to the floor. Sidling over to me, she leans down, holding out a glowing clear gem, it is mesmerising. 'I see the attraction.'

'Vi, don't stare at it.' Ash's words draw my attention.

Flynn holds up the gem like a trophy. 'Marry me, Ash; give me your perfect reputation as a cover for all my past faux pas.' She grins triumphantly. 'I have sent word to my father and when he arrives his beloved daughter shall be delivered to him and be out of harm's way and no longer destitute.'

'Why beat us?' Ash's eyes smoulder with anger.

My sister giggles. 'Fun and oh, a touch of jealousy. I saw the way you looked at her.'

Ash rolls his eyes. 'Yeah, sounds about right.'

She prances towards him, leaning down to him giving him a glance at another ample treasure. 'You have bulked up. Once a lanky youth who has now become a handsome, rugged man.'

'My companion is injured and has had a trying journey. Give us some time and I will consider your offer.'

Flynn pouts. 'Alone with her? No, I will leave my man servant Glenthon with you. Can't have you escaping, or worse, canoodling.' She points to a wine decanter on a side table near a luxurious looking bed. 'Help yourself. You have one hour before Lord Rueford Regallion arrives.' She hurries towards the exit, jewel in hand.

Rueford is my father's given name. Sweat beads on my brow I am *wanted.* By a father who has been searching for me. Heck, money, I could inherit some money and use it to restore Ash's home. My heart leaps with joy and I jump to my feet.

Tears slide down Ash's face as he strides towards me. So, it seems luck is against me as usual and will always be so. Joy will once more become a fleeting memory when he leaves me for her.

Chapter Ten

Ash joins me in three rapid strides. Glenthon moves away to stand beside the bed and pours himself a generous serve from the decanter into a shot glass. The room isn't large for noble suites and the smell of wine drifts towards me, heady with the scent of spring. I can almost taste the honey, grapes and hints of chamomile and lavender.

'Is that lachovine?' I stare at the decanter.

Glenthon nods and sips his drink.

Lachovine is common brew for the rich and is used to aid rest. It works quickly as the drink has a high alcohol content. I have always wanted to try it and if this is my only chance so be it. Ash reaches for me and I sidestep past him, knowing he intends to play the sacrifice. He will likely wed Flynn and hand me over to my so-called father, doing the noble duty of saving me.

'Pour me some.' I gesture to the decanter.

'Only one glass, miss,' Glenthon mutters.

I shrug. 'I care not, just do it.'

The man servant does as I bid and holds out the drink. I sip it, savouring the sweet, light brew. My inner turmoil lessens and I hold out the glass. 'Again.'

Glenthon obliges me and I down the contents and turn to Ash. 'So, you are going to marry Flynn, be the hero and also get what you want. Is that the gist?'

Spots of red spread across my friend's cheeks and he tugs at the collar of his shirt. 'Stuffy in here, I am going to open a window.'

The man servant begins to scull directly from the bottle. 'This is great stuff, can't afford it on what she pays me.'

Ash unlatches the windows decorated with a woodland scene, pushes them outwards and leans over the sill. He begins humming in what I assume is Valdarnish. Groaning, I hurry over to him and stare at his back.

'Ash, we need to say our farewells.'

He ignores my words and rage swells within. My stomach unleashes an unladylike cacophony and my cheeks burn as the unbidden gas exits rapidly. Glenthon erupts in hysterical laughter.

'Excuse me,' I mutter.

Ash turns, a grin on his face. 'Well, we've shared everything else, why not that?' He releases a loud belch.

I crane my head over my shoulder. Glenthon almost chokes on his wine and his stance is a little unsteady.

Ash leans towards me. 'Flynn is desperate and can hardly afford to employ the most professional of servants.'

'Seems so.'

His eyes soften. 'Do you love me, *Cevere*?'

'What does it matter now?' My shoulders tense.

'It matters a lot.'

I answer through gritted teeth and force out the words I am terrified to admit. 'I wouldn't say I don't.'

Ash reaches out and snatches my right hand and presses a kiss to the dorsal side. 'Good enough.'

My brow furrows. 'Why?'

'The church is where I will tie the knot and is at the back of the palace. I sent word to your father hours ago. Hopefully my message reaches him before Flynn's does. We have less than an hour, my love.'

He pulls me towards the window, lifts me in his arms and leans in for a kiss. 'She likes red.'

I close my eyes and certainly his kisses make me giddy but not like this. My eyes snap open; he has hoisted me over the ledge and before I can gather my wits my stomach drops as he lets me go. The rush of wind roars in my ears and I unleash an unearthly scream as I reach up an arm towards him. Ash smiles and chitters like some insect before he is pulled away from the window.

I close my eyes and turn midair with my face towards the ground. Shouts gather around me and a bell tolls like some presumptuous death knell. Then I am caught in some foul thing with sticky, flexible membranes. I touch my face and open my eyes to stare at my hands. I am alive. I sit up, white strands ripping away with me as I lean forward. I appear to be in some kind of giant web so big a terrifyingly large arachnid could possibly make it.

In the centre of this life-saving structure a gargantuan golden orb spider with a woman's face tilts its head towards me and chitters excitedly. I back away, shuffling towards the edge and stare downwards. I have dropped almost all the way down and look to be about fifty feet from the ground. I could jump from here but could easily break a leg or ankle.

The strange beast chitters again and I turn, staring wide-eyed as it gracefully climbs across the surface of its creation. The noises it makes are almost pleasant as if it is trying to soothe me and allay my fear. It continues on past me and turns its back end towards the outer webbing. The spider begins weaving, using its spindly hairy legs to form a rope-like ladder.

'Did Ash summon you?' I roll my eyes feeling quite foolish for talking to it.

She nods in understanding and I rummage around in my pockets, begin searching for a red stone and find a ruby. My chest tightens as I hold it up to the light. I toy with the idea of pushing her aside and keeping the gem. I am truly a selfish thing and dedicated kleptomaniac and it pains me to depart with more valuable plunder. But there is the matter of Ash. Sighing, I hold out the jewel. The spider creature smiles and I place the ruby on the web all the while fighting the urge not to throw up because of how eerie that smile is.

'Thank you.'

She hurries towards the jewel as I make use of the ladder, my hands becoming stickier as I descend. That ruby was valuable, but I have an even greater treasure to rescue. As my feet connect with the earth I fall to my knees and kiss the ground, spitting out dirt.

'Well, what a spectacular way to meet again.'

Scowling, I whirl around and stare up at a fae male dressed in finery; his blue hair matches my own but is long and braided down his back and jewels gleam amongst the silken strands. His nose is like my own. He cuts a handsome figure in Valdarnish attire that I have only heard of in stories. He is donned in finely spun pants made of some shimmering material that reach his bare feet, a silver belt is worn across his hips and a wicked looking knife has been slid into a loop on the side. He wears a simple, open vest made of silver fur and is bare-chested apart from the strap of a rough spun satchel worn off his left side.

'Ervina Owens?' He holds out a hand that I reach for and he pulls me to my feet.

'Lord Rueford Regallion, I presume.'

He winks. 'You could call me that or *Irin*.'

My forehead wrinkles. 'What does that mean?'

'Oh, you never learnt Valdarnish?'

I shake my head. 'Didn't seem necessary, people in Shaol were wary of my obvious fae blood.'

Rueford frowns. 'Well, in Valdarn all fae-born are welcome. Especially a future viscountess and Velshere whose gifts are met with praise. Unfortunately, our titles are almost useless amongst the human aristocracy and building a reputation takes a long time, hence my alter ego as a troubadour.' He smiles suddenly. 'Fae take a long time to get to the point as you will learn when you accompany me home. *Irin* means father in our tongue.'

I pull my hand from his. 'Where were you all this time?'

He wanders over to a grassy area and I follow. 'Sit, I will explain.' He lowers himself gracefully into a cross-legged position, poise being a trait only my sister must have inherited as I plop down without decorum.

'Ash has told me that you were estranged from a wife and fell for my mother and that she kicked you out.' I frown. 'If it is true, that is.'

'True.' He glances about. 'And where is your betrothed?'

I cock my head. 'Betrothed?'

His brows rise upwards. 'You are unaware?

'Obviously.'

He smiles, and his face lights up. When he smiles he is an outrageously handsome man that could easily sway almost anyone. 'I never liked the potential union between Flynn and Ash. My eldest is cold-hearted but follows the law tediously. Ash was a bit of a scoundrel in his youth. After his humiliation he wandered the countryside starting brawls, getting drunk and using magic to scare the more superstitious countryfolk. That is until I found him.'

I smile; the thought of Ash being a rogue warming my heart. Oh what we could do together, taking what we want and bringing revenge down on our haters. 'Then what happened?'

'I told him of you.' He brushes a curl behind my ears. 'Do you know of a mark on Ash's body? It is unusual in design.'

I nod. 'A half-moon shape on the inside of his left wrist.'

Rueford reaches for my right arm and flips it over. '*Dethorn Armagia.*'

My wrist burns as if the flesh is scalded and I wrench my hand away, blowing on the injury until a shape like Ash's birthmark appears on the raw flesh.

Put those together and you get a full moon.' My father sighs. 'I placed that spell to protect you from others. Have you heard the tale of the moon maiden?'

I glare. 'Who hasn't? And that hurt.'

He chuckles. 'You are terse like your mother.'

I shrug. 'And stubborn and wary like her too.'

'Was she good to you?'

I shake my head. 'Indifferent.'

'Well, that's a shame.' He stretches and hurries to his feet. 'Do you not have a fiancé to save?'

I give him a quizzical glance. 'Huh?'

He pulls a wrinkled scroll from his bag and unfurls it. His hand glimmers and he produces a magnificent sapphire quill. 'Ash has already signed the betrothal agreement; I have witnessed it. If you sign it no wedding can commence. He has told me all about you in a gushing letter, you are well suited. Oh and I have a present for Flynn for kidnapping a Valdarn noble.'

He grins as I reach for the writing implement; my hand trembles and I steady it with my other as I take the proffered item. 'Do I want this?'

My father's gaze softens. 'Only you can decide that, dear girl.'

Chapter Eleven

A bell tolls three times, letting me know my time is running out. I linger a distance behind my father who is accompanied by various fae people. His group includes grey, smooth-skinned folk; tiny faeries; and shambling swamp creatures who leave a foul-smelling, slippery trail in their wake.

Rueford and I had hastily formed a plan on the way over. He rejoins his travelling players and takes a silver flute from his satchel, bowing to a gathering crowd before he puts the instrument to his lips. He draws a few wispy, enchanting notes from the instrument as if he his coaxing out its very soul.

The players begin to frolic and oscillate, acting as if they are under some hidden spell. The memory of some ancient tune played by my cradle as an infant draws tears from my eyes. An elven woman in a diaphanous robe begins to sing. Her rich, vibrant voice soars above the melody, almost in reverence, as she sings the ode to Dornian.

We dwelt under a lightless sky once prey to the creatures that dwelleth there.

A guileless moon maiden innocent and bright took pity on our plight.

She lit the way for many a year until her lonely heart could take no more.

She turned her face towards the hills where a shepherd brandished blade before an injured boar.

The lad turned away and hurried down the hill returning to sheep, Dornian discerned his spirit was kind and meek.

The gift of the Salvane was given to him but he cast their love aside, disowning his future bride.

She took back what she was owed but a curse was imposed. Lonely until he shatters her fate and accepts her as his long lost mate.

We circle around the palace until we reach the back, and I deflect the light, slipping into the afternoon shadows as a servant hurries out of an open archway set into the wall. His eyes widen and he bows towards my father and his players. 'Are you here to entertain the wedding party?'

My father gives an exaggerated bow. 'I would wish my child well. Tell her I have received her message and would talk with her.'

A few sentries hurry towards Rueford, their hands hovering over their weapons. The movement of players and the gathered crowd prevent the guards' advancement. The distraction allows me to slip past and into the building.

The room is pretty standard and reminiscent of the faith hall in Shaol with its grey-painted walls and rough wooden benches. The universal symbol for the free worship of multiple deities, an inverted V, is painted on the stain glass window of the wall opposite the entrance. Sunlight filters through casting a shadow of the shape on to the polished, red tiled floor. A layperson dressed in a coarse brown linen tunic and felt shoes stands in front of a bubbling fountain.

These monuments are dedicated to the patron god of various regions and are found in chapels and places of worship all across Rersherdia. This one is made of white marble with a large harpoon fashioned from golden stone set in the middle. Water flows from a silver fish skewered atop the weapon and is likely dedicated to the god of fisherfolk known as Rivulet.

Ash turns, distracted by the increasing noise from the players outside. The servant from before hurries towards him. Flynn stands to his left facing the layperson and a middle-aged woman dressed in green robes dabs at her tearless eyes with a fine handkerchief. Ash's eyes sweep the room and his brow is lined with deep wrinkles.

Flynn turns to him. 'Looking for someone?'

Ash shakes his head and his shoulders slump. 'I guess not. Get on with it. But you agree we can live apart?'

Flynn purses her lips. 'As much as I hate it, I have agreed. Does your heart truly belong to her?'

The servant hurries over to my sister. 'Mistress, your father wishes to commune with you. He has received your message and would bless your union.'

Flynn turns to the servant, her eyes widening as the hint of a smile plays across her lips. She digs her nails into her palms as if she is distrusting of his words. Then it hits me; we both are the result of distant mothers and an absent father. A lonely and unfathomable road that comes with humiliation and the loss of hope and self-worth.

Whatever she has done Flynn has suffered a fate like mine only devoid of poverty. At least I could choose my fate. Beholden to her duties Flynn would have rebelled within the crushing confines of her noble burdens.

'I will see him.' Flynn turns towards the entrance as eagerness flashes in her eyes. The servant hurries away to relay his message to our father.

My heart softens and my need for revenge lessens as I shed myself of my invisibility. Glimmering on a green cloth on the edge of the fountain is the Salvane crystal. I slip towards it and reach down as Rueford enters the chapel with the servant.

My father bows almost mockingly towards the middle-aged woman. 'Wizardess Endorpha of Whitebrim Hall. Greetings, estranged wife.'

Endorpha's nostrils flare and she almost scoffs at my father. 'Lord Rueford Regallion renowned scoundrel and cad. Here to witness our child's wedding?'

My father shakes his head and sighs. 'Sadly it can't go ahead. Young Lord Asherton is engaged to the future Valdarn Viscountess Ervina Owens.'

Endorpha's eyes bulge and she shakes with alarming intensity. 'What proof do you have?'

Rueford retrieves the scroll and tosses it towards his wife who snatches it midair. She reads the document before glaring at her husband. 'Well, this is easily rectified.'

Ash turns to the estranged couple and stares at the exchange before his fist pumps the air. 'Vi loves me, she signed it.' He turns to face my sister, who has turned to stand between her parents. 'Keep your jewel. I am gaining the greatest treasure ever.'

'*Flareus*.' Endorpha clicks her fingers; a small flame appears and she lowers the scroll towards it.

'No!' I hurtle towards Flynn's mother and I am tackled by my sister. We fall to the floor in a tangle of skirts before she scratches my face with those manicured nails. I gasp before she grips my hair in a tiny fist and pulls. My head snaps backwards and I get a full view of her mother set on her evil task.

'Get your paws off him, you grimy pig-widgeon,' my sister all but screams.

'Flynn.' Endorphas's face turns an almost bright shade of perfect. 'Don't use the base words of commoners.'

My father produces a sharp burst on his flute and a gust of wind snatches the engagement contract up in a swift draft as Ash leaps forward and wrests it from the air.

'I'll have you for this.' Endorpha raises her hand outstretched before her husband. My father tilts his head towards the door and I thrust my sister away, bolting upright. The sound of weeping causes me to halt and I offer a hand to my sister as her eyes widen and a faint smile plays across her lips. 'You care?'

'I nod. 'Want to leave and let them work it out?'

My sister's hand snatches mine and I pull her to her feet. Ash grabs my other hand and we hasten towards the only exit.

'No. She stays, she has to answer for kidnapping.' My father smiles sadly.

Endorpha points at me. '*Scourges magnificio.*'

A sound of a cracking whip almost deafens me and then, like a strike from that very weapon, my right shoulder burns. A tear forms in my sleeve and an angry red welt appears. My father retaliates and Ash slams into me from behind; his body sheltering me and he flings and arm across Flynn's shoulder. 'Stay down, both of you.'

A harsh sound from the flute causes me to glance up. Tiny orbs flashing with lightning hover in the air above my father who then positions himself like a graceful crane. He begins to twirl on one leg causing his long braid to whip around him like some gigantic, adorned tassel. The jewels in his hair sparkle before he lands on two feet and pushes his arms out towards his nemesis. The orbs of lightning hurtle towards her.

Endorpha screams and raises her arms to cover her face. '*Batellis.*' Oil gushes onto the floor from under her skirts and spreads outwards towards Rueford. My father loses his footing and his estranged wife clicks her fingers.

'No!' I wriggle underneath Ash as desperation floods my senses. I won't be able to warn my father in time.

The floor catches alight and the flames spread rapidly as if fanned from an unnatural source. Ash pushes himself off us and fumbles for the book in his pocket. He snaps back the leather cover and begins thumbling through the pages. I pull the Salvane crystal from my pocket and hold it out to him. He turns to a page and grips the crystal above his head in his other hand. 'Rivulet blessed.'

The crystal glows causing Ash's eyes to sparkle as if lit within by magic and the crystal chimes in response to his words. Water is redirected from the fountain and rains down upon us, dousing the flames and producing a drenched and angry looking Endorpha.

Rueford breaks out into laughter and I join in as the stress of the last few days finally catches up with me.

My sister pushes herself to her feet and gives me an apologetic smile. 'Keep him.' Before she hurries past my father and out the door.

'I'll deal with you later,' my father shouts after her.

Ash drops the book back into his pocket and his arms encircle me as I rest my head on his shoulder and he hands me the crystal. 'A gift of a pledge between us.'

Chapter Twelve

Drenched, covered in grime and slick with oil and my hair sporting some trendy new patches, I rub my sore shoulder.. It could be worse; I could have died eaten by a bizarre monster or succumbed to a deadly fall. Or worse yet been engulfed in deadly flames seems like a horrid way to go. I'll take the grime and the pain knowing I'll live another day. The guards arrested Endorpha and Rueford for violence in a sacred space. Flynn has fled and I guess is on the run. Maybe I will meet her again one day.

Ash sits beside me on a park bench. A couple of reporters have spent the last hour barraging us with questions.

'So, Miss Owens. What was it like to meet your father again after all these years?' asks a swarthy individual dressed in a fashionable gown.

'Sod off.' Ash glares at her.

'I think we are done here.' The woman turns on her heel and leaves.

The crowd disperses with her, giving us a moment of breathing space.

The magistrate who had called the guard assured us both my father and his wife may lose their life for such a sacrilegious act. I must get word to my sister to save her mother.

I turn to my fiancé. 'I want to travel to the fae lands with my father, but first we have to free him.'

Ash caresses my cheek with his thumb. 'When do we start?'

I hold out the crystal before the man I love, his hand closes over mine. 'Keep it.'

'But you will need it for the upcoming journey.'

He smiles and his eyes light up. 'Who needs power when I have you? Marry me, Vi.'

My eyes widen. 'But I am a nobody.'

He pulls me in for an embrace his head resting on my shoulder. 'Not to me.' Ash draws back, pressing a kiss to my forehead. 'I vow to love you even when we bicker.' His lips caress my cheek. 'To provide for you before myself.' He presses his mouth to my neck. 'I promise to be the shelter, the family, that you have been searching for.'

A sob catches in my throat. 'Ash, I am just a lowly rogue. Yes, I will have money but no title befitting marriage to a noble in these lands.'

His mouth brushes mine. 'A thief who stole my heart. I love you. Don't deny yourself happiness.'

Turmoil wars for control. Can I take a chance at happiness and burden this man with me? I glance up and his eyes brim with love and I see no indecision there.

'I will marry you. I love you too.' I brush the tears out of my eyes as my hand shakes. I open my closed fist and drop the crystal. It floats up into the air and shatters causing a cascade of crystal flakes to fall from the sky like shards of hardened moonlight.

A distant memory of a shepherd kissing a lonely moon maiden flitters across my mind and I stare at Ash. My soul bursts with joy forcing a giddy thrill to pulse through me and I break out into bouts of laughter.

'The curse is broken,' I mutter breathlessly after my laughter has faded.

'Would seem so, *Cevere*.' He traces my mouth with a finger. 'My beautiful moon maiden, my mate.'

Pain courses through my heart like it is full and yet shattering at the same time. It is like I am falling from the heavens only to be caught in the arms of a kindly shepherd. A long distant memory, yet the pain and glory of it fills me now.

Ash's eyes are filled with bewilderment and he clutches at his chest. 'Mates; I thought that was a myth. Why does it hurt so much?'

'Because our love was overwhelming. My shepherd has guided me back to him.' My voice cracks as the pain and shock subsides. 'You didn't forget me.'

'In our last life I searched for you until my last days hoping you would forgive me and yet you eluded me. This lifetime we have both found each other.' He begins to sob before he pulls me into his arms. His presence is everything. I am finally home.

The End

Lord Willaford Bexley Asherton the Fifth
of Fishluck Hall & Ervina Owens.

About the author

Ima Ghoul enjoys breaking confines, offering stories that encourage the reader to interact, and writes quirky short stories full of hilarity and heart. Able to write across multiple genres, Ima has put her pen to works in sci-fi, mild horror, fantasy and closed-door romances.

Ima first knew she wanted to be a writer when she would make up bold games as a child and enact them out with her siblings. She enjoys long walks amongst ancient trees as it is grounding to her wild soul, and loves archery and role playing games. Her home is a place of organised chaos with three children, a hubby and five chickens as she adores animals, especially birds and deer.

Ima once had a fascination for pig latin and her love of deer lead to her gamer tag AwnFay. This new interest encouraged her to create her own languages as a kid and plays a big part in her fantasy writing under her other pen name. An avid reader first, Ima devours tomes in a day then spends hours reminiscing over them.

Her first novella Zombies & Papercuts started out as a fun little activity and feedback from a reader encouraged her to write a sequel. This has lead to her writing more short stories and closed-door romances which she has found she has a knack for and hopes to share her joy for writing them with her readers.

Also by Ima Ghoul

Zombies & Papercuts

Would you believe it I am Would you believe it I am thirty-three and have never been pashed? Let me introduce myself, my name is Alara and I am a librarian in a small country town in South Australia and a local nobody. As my luck would have it, doom coincides with my birthday and the party guests happen to be zombies.

But I am an eternal optimist. Will today be the day I finally share my first kiss? Armed only with my wit and books let's hope I don't get a papercut. They hurt more than a zombie bite.

Weird & Wacky Anthology: Volume One

Delve into the the wacky, the witty and mildly creepy, from tales of magic, aliens and ghouls to sweet romances.

Ima Ghoul, author of Zombies and Papercuts, brings the adventurous reader an anthology of short stories that won't fail to tantalise and amuse.

Will you cross the threshold?

Turn the page ... I dare you!

Zombies & Cricket

The night fills with the familiar chirp of crickets and the irritating hum of mozzies. I swat at one. My chest tightens as I lick my lips, trying to will away the intrusive thought, and now guilty pleasure, of wondering if mozzies have edible brains. So, it is happening, and relatively fast.

After the zombie apocalypse, the government found a temporary solution and encouraged us to continue living our lives. Let me introduce myself. My name is Gavin, a 43-year-old cattle farmer from South Australia, with a love of cricket. As the one−year anniversary−now aptly named Use Your Noggin Day−and my gal's birthday, approaches, there has been an increase in zombie attacks.

Will I be able to protect Alara, keep my humanity
and still play the match next weekend?

www.ingramcontent.com/pod-product-compliance
Lightning Source LLC
Chambersburg PA
CBHW070448170726
48291CB00005B/1644